THE UNWILLING LOVE

L. STEELE

L. Steele

WELCOME TO PRIMROSE HILL

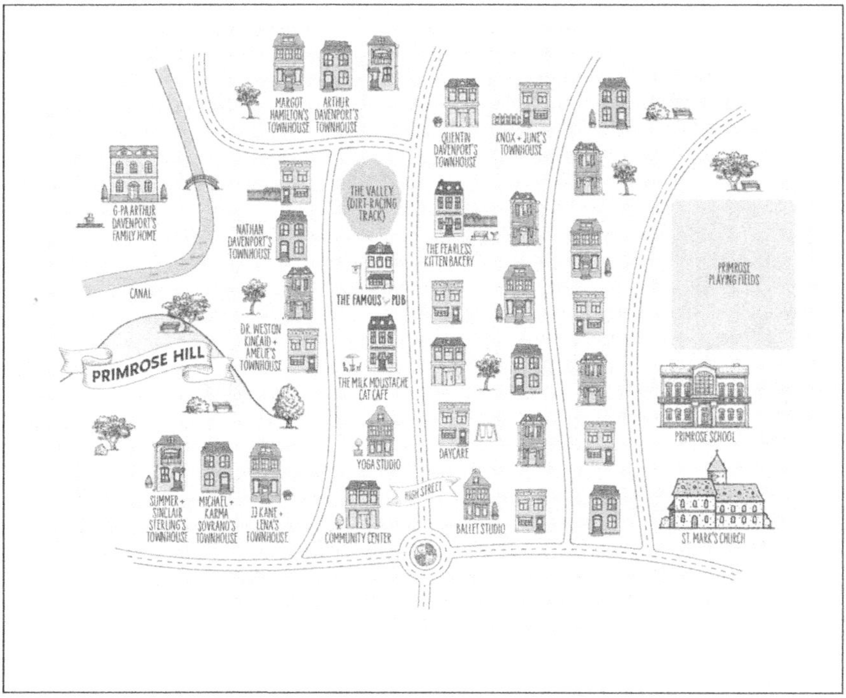

THE HAMILTONS

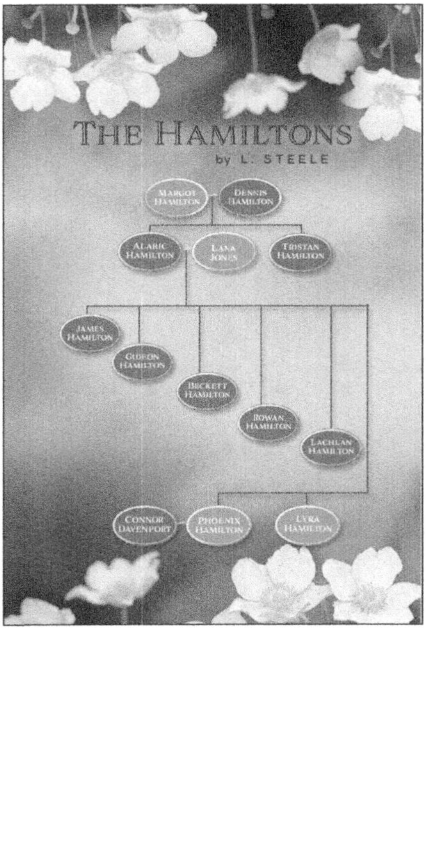

THE DAVENPORTS

HARPER AND JAMES

JAMES AND HARPER

DEDICATION

For the good girls
who secretly love a man
who looks at you once

and decides

"you're mine."

I see you

1

THIS IS THE PREQUEL TO THE UNWILLING BRIDE, HAMILTONS #1, BY L. STEELE

Harper

"What's he doing here?" My friend, Phoenix stares over my shoulder.

"Who are you talking about?" I turn to look.

"Don't do that!" She grabs my hand and drags me to the dance floor. "My oldest brother is here." She has to shout to be heard above the music.

"James?" I stiffen. "Isn't he on tour?"

I've heard about Phe's older brother. He's a decorated Marine away on missions so classified only select members of His Majesty's government knows the details. I've never met him before.

"He's supposed to be on leave starting next week." Phe gyrates to the beats. "He must have returned earlier than planned. He's not going to be pleased to see me here."

Ah, so that's why she's elbowing her way through the crush of bodies.

"You are twenty-one," I scoff. "Surely, you can do as you please?"

She snorts. "Tell that to my overprotective sibling. James is the oldest, and the most controlling of them."

She's the youngest of seven. And five of them are brothers. I wince. "Damn, it's not easy when you're the youngest, huh?"

"You can say that again."

Soon, we're in the middle of the sweaty, moving mass of people on the dance floor.

The DJ amps up the beats, and the boom-boom-boom of the rave music seems to ricochet off my ribcage and bang against my heart. My bones seem to rattle. My ear drums clog. For a few seconds, I'm one with the music. I shake my booty, grinding up against Phoenix, who giggles, then mirrors my moves. The two of us turn so we're back-to-back, dancing up and down against each other. The man opposite me sways his hips, flashes his smile, and gyrates in synchronicity with me. I laugh, feeling young and carefree and happy. I'm a year into my degree in hospitality management and working part time in a restaurant.

The future feels wide open. Like I am straddling so many beginnings, I have no idea which one I'm going to choose.

The beats pump up even further. I bounce up and down, up and down, giving over to the sheer delight of becoming one with the music.

Phoenix laughs out loud and mirrors me.

The two of us hold hands and sing aloud with the words that pump out in between the notes. The DJ switches off the music, and for a few seconds, it's just us, our voices, and the voices of those around us. In harmony. We sound as one. That primal feeling of taking part in a group activity and being linked to a community who, for this second at least, feels like they're connected to me.

Then, the beats restart. The music slices through the space, bangs into my ears, and thrums across my pulse points.

I reach into a place deep inside and pull on the energy that lurks just below the surface. Adrenaline pumps into my blood. I move my legs, my arms, my hips even faster. Close my eyes and give myself up on the altar of the beats. Spin around. And around, the lights flashing behind my closed eyelids. Drop deep into a part of me lost to the trance. Hear Phe say something but can't catch it. Spin again. Trip. And pitch forward.

Only, I'm stopped by hands which grip my biceps.

A shiver zips out from the point of contact. I snap my eyes open, taking in the tanned skin exposed by the lapels of the man standing in front of me. The white of the shirt stands out in relief. He's wearing a jacket which clings to his broad shoulders. He cuts out the sight of everything behind him.

He tightens his hold on me. I tip my head back, and further back, until my gaze is caught by the electric blue eyes which seem to crackle with displeasure, and something else. An awareness that sizzles between us, so visceral it turns the air heavy, until I can taste it on my tongue. My throat goes desert dry.

I swallow, but it's useless. The tension wraps around my windpipe like a fist.

His thick eyebrows draw down. Along with his hooked nose and the scar over one cheekbone, it adds to the air of danger clinging to him.

It also hugely adds to his appeal. I'm aware, I'm staring. That I'm, somehow, rooted to the spot and, apparently, unable to take my gaze off his very striking good looks. He must notice it too, for his lips thin.

His jawline tightens. A slash of disapproval cuts through the haze I seem to have fallen into. Anger radiates off of him. It adds to his dark handsomeness. The sense of lethal confidence that ebbs and flows around him.

My breathing speeds up, my pulse rate dancing in tandem with the beats that vibrate the air around me.

The attraction between us snaps tighter, drawing us into a cocoon of need that cuts us off from the rest of the crowd. The music seems to fade. The people around us disappear. It's just me and this dangerous stranger, and the electricity holding us in thrall.

He rakes his gaze across my face and seems fascinated by my mouth. My core trembles. My stomach tightens. Butterflies erupt in my blood stream. Oh my god. This intense awareness of him is like nothing I've ever experienced.

He must feel the pull, for a flush streaks across his cheekbones. His gaze narrows. He begins to lower his head, and as if in a dream, I go up on tiptoes. His face is inches from mine, close enough for me to make out the lines radiating from his eyes. His irises are vivid, an intense, almost unnatural, glacial blue. They should seem cold, but right now, they burn as if lit from within by an electrical storm.

My breath catches. My heartbeat spikes. I part my lips, anticipating the kiss when—

"James." Phe steps around me. "What are you doing here?"

James

I jump back as if I've been burned. So does she.

I take in her big green eyes, that blonde hair gathered in a saucy ponytail which bounces as she moves. As for her hourglass figure, I've been itching to run my fingers over her curves since I saw her on the dance floor.

Watching her grind those luscious hips and throw her head back, laughing and moving to the music... It made me want to stomp over and plant my body in front of her so no one else can see that gorgeous body.

The possessiveness takes me by surprise. I don't normally want to both protect a woman and haul her into my bed at the same time. It's a strange combination of tenderness and lust, which sets alarm bells ringing in my head.

Not to mention, my response is all wrong. She's my sister's friend. That's not a relationship I want to mess up. And that's exactly what will happen if I act on this impulse to throw this woman over my shoulder and carry her out of here to have my way with her.

I'd enjoy her and then, I'd be done with her. And that would make things very uncomfortable between them. She's too innocent for the likes of me. I've seen war, killed men, and buried friends. The nightmares I've seen and the darkness I carry inside of me as a result would only taint her. It's best I leave her alone.

I'm very aware of my sister waiting for my response. But despite my best efforts, it takes me a few more seconds to rip my gaze from her friend's beautiful face and to my sister. "Question is, what are *you* doing here?'

I have to raise my voice to be heard above the music, but Phe hears it. So does her friend. *What is she doing here, surrounded by men who've been eyeing her since she stepped onto the dance floor?*

One of them bumps into her.

I glare at the numbskull. He pales, stumbles back. Aiming a last 'keep off' scowl at him, I turn to Phe. "It's time for you to get home."

Her friend stiffens.

Phe rolls her eyes. "Seriously? We just started dancing."

I bark out a laugh. "Nice try, Squirt. You've been on the dance floor for close to an hour."

"But I want to dance all night long," she whines.

"The music is too good to leave now," her friend protests.

I allow myself to look at her, once more taking in those sparkling green eyes and the thick blonde hair framing her features. Instantly, that attraction I feel toward her snaps tight.

It doesn't matter that we're surrounded by gyrating people or that my sister is watching the two of us with curiosity. She's probably picking up on the chemistry between us, which makes me uncomfortable. It's bad taste to hit on my little sister's friend.

Yet I'm helpless in the face of the attraction between us.

My pulse races, my muscles are so tense they seem to have turned into granite. My skin prickles with the need to have contact with hers.

Every instinct within me pushes me to haul her off the dance floor and away from the peering eyes of those around her.

I curl my fingers into fists to prevent myself from reaching out to touch her. I'm ashamed that I'm unable to resist this draw to her.

Me, the Marine who's proud of my iron self-control, yet I'm helpless in the face of my attraction toward this woman.

I shake my head to clear it. I must be more deprived than I realized. Being on back-to-back tours of duty can do that to a man.

It's only the possibility that I'd lose my sister's trust not to mention my own self-respect and honor, if I act on my baser instincts towards her friend which spurs me on to finally rein in my desires.

I square my shoulders, keep my eyes averted from my sister's friend.

"Can we have this discussion where my eardrums don't feel like they're being shredded?" I plead with Phe.

"You're so old," my sister yells in my ear.

That I am. Older than her, that is. I give her my best big brother stare.

It works, for she throws up her hands. "Whatever." Phe pivots and begins to elbow her way through the gyrating masses.

I step around and in front of her, shouldering people aside. In seconds, we're out of the sweaty, heat of the dance floor.

I draw in gulps of breath, glance over my shoulder to make sure the girls are following me, then head toward a relatively quieter corner of the bar. I find a high-top table and lean my elbow on it.

First Phe, then her gorgeous friend reach the table.

"You're such a bore," Phe whines.

I lean over and tug her hair. "And you've turned into a regular party animal."

"Dancing for an hour, on a crowded dance floor at"—she pulls out her phone and pretends to check the time—"eleven pm makes me a party animal. Not," Phe coughs.

Her friend stays silent.

Phe turns to her. "What do you think?"

She looks between us. "I'm not getting involved."

Phe throws her arm around her friend. "Oh, you're involved, all right, girlfriend. We're here because *you* wanted to go dancing."

I scowl at her friend. I saw her dancing, all right.

The way she shook her arse, rotated her hips, and twirled around on her toes mesmerized me. The lights bounced off her, covering her in a shimmering aura which made her seem almost otherworldly.

And damn, if I wasn't drawn to her. Watching her shake her booty turned my dick to stone, and my balls felt like boulders. I also noticed how every other man in the room seemed to be focused on her. It made me want to step over and tear their eyes out. The level of possessiveness I felt—still feel—about her is bewildering.

Some of my feelings must show on my face, for her gaze widens. She holds out her hand. "I'm Harper. Harper Richie."

"Oh, I'm sorry, I didn't realize you two haven't been introduced." Phoenix waves her hand between us. "Harper, this is James, my brother. James… This is my bestie, Harper."

I take Harper's much smaller palm in mine.

A current of electricity zips up my arm. The hair on the nape of my neck rises. Holy hell. What kind of a crazy response am I having to this woman?

No, she's a girl. And she's out of bounds. Also, what is she wearing?

Why is her dress so short? Enough to bare her creamy thighs. Combined with her boots and her high ponytail, they make her look sexy yet also, sweet.

I can't help but imagine wrapping her ponytail around my hand and urging her to her knees. Then I'd yank on her hair, so she opens her mouth, enough for me to ease my cock between those lips and—I shove aside the images my thoughts have conjured. Take a few deep breaths to try to dispel the tightness at my crotch. *'Try' being the operative word.*

I get my thoughts under control and focus on my sister. And because I can't ask this question of Harper, I aim it at Phe. "What are you wearing?"

She looks down at herself. "I'm wearing a perfectly respectable mini-dress which is—"

"Miniscule." I fold my arms across my chest. "I understand, you're grown up. You're an adult. But don't expect me to be in the same room and watch you"—I nod in the direction of the dance floor—"make an exhibition of yourself."

"Nobody asked you to come here and watch," mumbles Harper.

The girls laugh, and I give them a quelling look.

Two men pass by, both eying Phe and Harper in a way that makes my stomach bottom out.

Yes, I've been to bars. Yes, I've looked at women with only one thing in mind. The same thing that these wankers are thinking about.

I glare at them. One of them looks at me and pales. The other one catches my eye and scowls. He comes to a stop. I draw myself up to my full height and slap my arms on my hips. When I thrust out my chest, the bastard swallows. His friend pulls on his arm, and the two walk away in a rush.

Good. I relax a little.

My urge to whisk her out of here is... Only because I'm a gentleman. Though my thoughts about *her* are far from gentlemanly.

Phe tosses her head. "Jeez, if you keep looking like that at anyone who passes us, we'll never find anyone to dance with."

I smirk. *That's the idea.* But I don't say that aloud.

"You've spoiled our evening." Her lips turn down.

My chest tightens. Damn, I'm such a softie for my sister.

And very hard for her friend.

I keep my gaze averted from Harper, walk around, and wrap my arm around Phe. I kiss her forehead. "When I'm not around, I'm sure you get up to all kind of shenanigans. But I can't stop myself from being protective. So, humor me, okay?"

And why do I feel so territorial about her friend? It's a question to which I'm not sure I want to know the answer.

She sighs, then throws up her hands. "Fine." She glances at Harper. "You okay to get out of here?"

2

Harper

It's early, and I do want to dance. *I want to do the horizontal with her brother even more.* Ugh. Wonder how Phe would react if I told her that I find her brother attractive? Perhaps, she wouldn't mind? But I do feel guilty that I'm eyeing my best friend's brother like he's a slice of tiramisu I'd love to devour layer by layer.

James watches me from under hooded eyes. His jaw is set. He lowers his arm from around Phe and surveys me with an impatient look.

It's as if he expects to be obeyed. I have a good mind to tell him that he's not my keeper. That I'll do as I damn well please. Although, if I'm being honest, there's a part of me that would like for him to boss me around. But the last thing I want is to make things difficult for Phe.

She widens her gaze at me, a pleading look in her eyes.

I sigh, then nod almost imperceptibly at her.

James spots it though, for his shoulders relax slightly. He hustles the two of us toward the hallway. He's tall and broad, with shoulders wide enough that the crowd parts before us.

We retrieve our coats and button up, before following him up the stairs and onto the street.

Cool air engulfs me. I welcome it after the cloying heat of the club. I take in lungfuls, tucking strands of hair that have come loose behind my ears.

"This way." James leads us to a Jeep Wrangler parked a few cars down. A beep sounds as he unlocks the doors. He holds the front door open.

Phe bypasses it, wrenches the back door open, and climbs in.

It's either climb into the passenger seat or appear impolite. I can't quite give word to the reasons why I'd rather not sit in the passenger seat next to James. I can't exactly say aloud that if I sit that close to him, I'm going to be affected by his nearness. That he feels larger than life, and so handsome, and extremely hot. Enough to distract me. That I feel a certain nervousness around him. And I'm worried that I might give away how he unnerves me.

He holds the door open, looking at me with curiosity.

"You okay, Harper?" Phe calls out from the back of the car.

I laugh. "Just trying to enjoy a few last minutes of cool air."

Without giving myself a chance to second guess myself, I climb into the Jeep, trying and failing not to draw in a quick sniff of the dark scent that emanates from James. A very male scent. Salt combined with a whiff of metal, and leather infused with notes of cedar. It's a scent that hints at the danger the man carries pressed into his skin. It screams that he can't be tamed. That he's someone who lives a very different life from mine.

He's a Marine who's seen his share of action on the frontline, accordingly to what Phe has told me.

"All right?" His low voice rumbles over me.

I shiver, then lock my fingers together in my lap and nod.

He searches my features, then reaches for the seatbelt and hands it to me. "Don't forget to buckle in." He smirks at my flustered expression, then glances in the backseat. "You too, Phe."

He shuts the door, rounds the Jeep, and just before he slides into the driver's seat, Phe grumbles, "Bossy."

He eases the car forward onto the street.

"Drop me off first, and then you can take Harper home," Phe calls out from behind.

I whip my head around, surprised and more than a little flustered by her suggestion. "What?! No, I... I don't want to trouble him—"

"No trouble," he cuts me off.

I frown. "You could drop me off at the tube station and—"

"It's eleven p.m. I'm seeing you home." His voice brooks no argument.

I firm my lips and stop the sharp retort hovering at the tip of my tongue. I'm in his vehicle. I don't want to seem impolite. Also, I don't want to make it awkward for Phe.

Still, I can't stop myself from glaring at her.

She holds up her hands. "You don't have to accept the lift if you don't want to."

James stiffens. I sense the disapproval radiating from him. But to his credit, he stays quiet.

"I just don't think it's safe for you to call a car at this late hour." She widens her eyes. "And I live closer, so it makes sense for James to drop me off first. That's why I sat in the back."

Oh, you've got to be kidding me.

She's playing cupid. And she's not being subtle about it.

Phe picked up on the chemistry between us and now she's orchestrating this like some meddling matchmaker who thinks she knows what's best for everyone.

Heat crawls up my neck. The *mortified* kind.

If James figures out what she's doing, and he's not an idiot, he's going to think I put her up to this. That I'm some desperate girl who needs her best friend to manufacture alone time with him. He'll shut down completely, and any chance I have of him seeing me as anything other than his little sister's pathetic friend will evaporate.

I shoot Phe a look that promises retribution. A *long* conversation about boundaries and interfering in my love life. She has the audacity to give me an innocent smile.

We're going to have words later.

But what choice do I have? Refusing the ride makes this into a bigger thing than it already is. Makes it obvious that I *am* affected by him, that sitting alone in a car with James Hamilton is dangerous territory.

I grit my teeth. "Fine." I nod in James' direction without looking at him. "Thank you for the ride."

My tone is grudging, but I refuse to mask it. I turn and busy myself looking out the window, remaining silent.

We drive for a few minutes. Slowly, my muscles unwind, enough for me to sneak a peek in his direction.

The lights from passing cars and streetlights sweep over his face like a spotlight interrogating secrets.

The hollows under his cheekbones carve deeper with each flash, lending a brutal handsomeness to his profile that shouldn't be as appealing as it is. Light, dark, light, dark. The rhythm is hypnotic.

In the brightness, I catch the fine lines around his eyes, proof of laughter I've never heard, a warmth I've never seen. Then shadow devours him whole, turning him back into sharp angles and that stern, unforgiving mouth that could wreck me. Intimidating as hell. Beautiful as sin. Two versions of the same man, and I want them both. Both dangerous. Both capable of destroying me in different ways.

"You never told us what you were doing at the club," Phe calls out from the seat behind us.

James glances at the rearview mirror. "I was supposed to meet a friend."

"A friend?" Phe frowns.

Was he meeting a date? Somehow, the thought makes my heart sink, and I'm not sure why. I don't know this man at all. I've only just met him, yet I feet this attraction to him. This pull I've never experienced before. Enough for me to ask, "A girlfriend?"

No sooner are the words out than I wince. Why did I blurt that out? It hints at the direction my thoughts have taken. And I don't want him to find that out. When his lips twist though, I realize, I'm not in luck.

"A *friend*," he drawls.

I shoot a glance at his face, but he's focused on the road.

"Hmph." I place my hands in my lap and turn to gaze through the windshield as well.

"You don't have a girlfriend though, do you?" Phe's voice is casual. *Too casual.*

I flush to the roots of my hair. Argh, she's asking the questions I can't. She's taking this matchmaking thing too seriously.

And James has definitely noticed, for when he replies, he addresses her but turns to me. "No, I don't."

Our gazes clash, hold, and then I forget to be embarrassed because by God, every pore in my body seems to pop. Something sizzles in the air between us and envelops us in a cocoon of bubbling intimacy. The rest of the world fades. Electricity zips down my spine and to my extremities.

Then, he turns back to the road. The bubble pops. I release the breath I wasn't aware I was holding.

Now that he's not looking at me, some of the tension in my muscles fades. But being in this enclosed space with him means I'm still very aware of him.

"What happened to your friend?" Surely, my words must reveal that I'm interested in him. But I can't stop myself. That secret part of me that awakened when I saw him wants to elongate this conversation, just so I can be at the receiving end of his attention.

"I told him I had something important come up," he murmurs.

"What are you doing back in town? I thought you weren't on leave for another week," Phe asks.

Tension snaps through him. I glance at him in time to see him set his jaw. "Our mission wrapped up early, so I came home." A muscle ticks above his cheekbone.

Something tells me, that's not all to the story.

Phe, too, must pick up on the heaviness that seems to wrap around him, for she doesn't push him for clarification. We fall silent for a few seconds, then she murmurs, "It's good to have you home, big brother. Even though you can be a pain in the you-know-where, by being overprotective."

He shoots her a grin in the mirror, and my breath catches. James Hamilton smiling is a punch to the gut.

The charisma rolls off him like heat from an oven set to broil, inescapable in close quarters. His presence hums with a low magnetic pull. An allure I feel in my bones, the way you feel a timer about to go off before it rings. My heart stutters. My thighs tremble. This man is a force of nature. The kind that diverts the direction of rivers and causes volcanoes to erupt.

My mouth is suddenly dry. I wrap my arms about myself in an attempt to get control of my emotions. The sudden movement catches his attention.

He swivels his head in my direction, his gaze tangling with mine, and I feel it in every cell in my body.

A flush colors my cheeks. My pussy clenches. It's as if he's sucked out all the oxygen in the car, and I can't breathe. Then he looks away, and once again, I feel like I've been released from the web of a spider. He turns off the road and onto a side street. A few minutes later, he's pulling up in front of Phe's home.

He brings the car to a stop, pulls up the handbrake, then throws his arm over the back of his seat and turns to look at her. "It's good to see you too, squirt."

Phe wrinkles her nose. "That makes me feel ten again. And I'm not anymore. You know that, right?"

His feature soften. "You'll always be ten to me."

Phe rolls her eyes, leans forward and drops a kiss on his cheek. "Bye, Mr. Royal Marine. Thanks for the ride. Goodnight, Harper." She winks, then pushes her door open and steps out. He waits until she's safely inside of her apartment building. She turns and waves at us, then shuts the door.

For a few seconds, we sit in silence, then he turns to me. "What's your address?"

3

Harper

"You really don't have to drop me at home."

He grunts. "I told Phe I'd drop you home, and I will." His voice is firm, his stance immovable.

"Damn, you're a smooth talker, huh?" I narrow my gaze on him.

His lips twitch.

I do believe I coaxed a smile out of him. Maybe, there's hope, after all.

I tell him my address, and he keys it in. Then he eases the car onto the road. Somehow, he's driving me home, despite my best efforts to put him off. I have a feeling, once James Hamilton puts his mind to something, he always gets his way.

A few seconds later, he leans over and touches the screen on the dash. The Wrangler has clearly been fitted with upgraded tech.

The strains of classical music fill the space.

I look at him in surprise.

"You don't seem like a classical music kinda guy."

He tilts his head.

"Figured you more for rock or country, maybe."

He scoffs.

I wait for him to elaborate further. When he doesn't, I add, "Country music because you drive a Jeep, you know?"

"Hmph." He slows to a stop at a traffic light.

He grips the steering wheel with those broad hands, and I can see the tension in every tendon, the white-knuckle hold of a man barely keeping himself in check. His spine is straight, shoulders square, jaw locked tight. He stares straight ahead like he's facing down an enemy instead of an empty intersection. His profile could have been carved from stone, all harsh angles and unforgiving lines, beautiful in the way a professional chef's knife is beautiful. Dangerous. Sharp enough to draw blood if you get too close. And God help me, I want to.

"Something to compliment your rugged, smoldering, intense personality." Not sure why I blurt that out. Heat sears my cheeks.. My words give away that I've been studying him and forming an opinion about him. Which I have. But telling him so makes me feel vulnerable.

Maybe he won't notice? But his next words disavow me of that notion.

"You came to that conclusion in the little time you spent with me?" he rumbles.

When I dart another look at his face, it's to find his expression unreadable. I frown. His lack of expression makes it difficult to understand what kind of impact my words have on him.

"You're right, I may have come to a premature conclusion."

He grunts.

Which I take to mean that he agrees with me. Or maybe, not.

Difficult to say when the man prefers to communicate with noises instead of words.

"I could, of course, get to know you better." I cringe. Did I say that aloud? I must have lost the connection between my brain and my mouth.

There's silence. The traffic lights change to green. He eases the car forward.

When he doesn't reply, I squirm in my seat. This tall, dark, brooding, and silent persona of his makes me want to keep talking to fill in the gap. I manage not to… For a full minute.

Then I add, "Forget I said that. I didn't mean it."

No reply.

"I mean, I did mean it. But of course, you don't have to spend time with me. It's just… As you pointed out, I seem to have come to some conclusions which might not be accurate, so I thought it would be best if—"

"Okay."

I stare at him. Did I hear him wrong? "Did you say—"

"Ice cream," he snaps out.

"Excuse me?"

"Do you like ice cream?"

"Who doesn't? But what's that got to do with anything?"

He flips the indicator, slows down, then comes to a stop in front of an ice cream shop at the side of the road. One that's still open and popular, judging by the people inside.

"Ah, ice cream." Right. Again, not what I expected him to suggest. Or to pull up right away. Another way I've misjudged him, apparently.

When his lips twist, I realize he, too, must think the same.

He smirks. Then shoves his door open and steps out. I reach for my door handle, but he's already rounded the car and opens it for me.

"Thanks." I step out. He shuts the door and guides me with an impersonal touch at the small of my back. Doesn't stop the goosebumps from peppering my skin.

We reach the shop, and he pushes the door open, then follows me in. He heads for the ice cream display case.

The woman behind it, who must be in her late twenties, stops what she was doing and walks over to him. "How can I help?" She gives him a big smile. Ugh, what a ho.

He turns to me, a question in his eyes.

I have the satisfaction of seeing her face fall.

"Strawberry and mango for me, please. In a cone. With sprinkles. And also, chocolate sauce."

"Of course." She tears her gaze off James' face with obvious reluctance, then picks up a cone and proceeds to create my order.

She hands it over. Then turns to James and bats her eyelashes. "And what can I get you?"

A small smile plays around his lips. "A couple of scoops of your bitter chocolate ice cream. In a cup, please."

Instantly, a hot sensation squeezes my chest. Nah, I can't be jealous because he smiled at another woman? Also, bitter chocolate? Of course, that'd be the flavor he'd go for.

"Anything else?" She makes googly eyes at him. How obvious can she get? I resist the urge to snort.

"No, I'm good." He doesn't seem aware of how she's angling to get his attention.

Man has no idea he's a lethal, walking sex-machine, laying low any woman within a mile of his overwhelming presence.

She scoops the ice cream into a cup and hands it over.

"Thank you." He takes it from her.

"No, thank *you*." She holds onto the ice cream cup for a few more seconds than is strictly necessary, in my totally unbiased opinion.

When she finally let's go, she flutters her eyelids. Jeez, is this woman for real?

She opens her mouth to ask something else, and I step in closer to James, enough to brush his arm with mine.

"Thanks. How much is that?"

"I've got it." James pulls out his phone and taps it against the credit card reader she holds up.

With another nod in her direction, he pockets his phone, spins around, and heads for the door. He holds it open for me, then follows me out.

"You didn't have to pay for my ice cream."

He ignores me and unlocks the vehicle. Then walks around to hold the passenger door open for me. I slide in. He shuts the door, rounds the car and gets into the driver's seat.

He holds up the cup of ice-cream and takes a bite out of it.

"You could have gotten a cone."

"Eh?" He frowns.

"You're eating from the cup like it's a cone. You could have gotten a cone."

He gives me a funny look, then takes a second bite out of the ice cream in his cup.

Only he would make eating ice cream into a competitive sport of manliness. I roll my eyes. "Right, that would have put a dent in that silent, macho thing you have going on, eh?"

4

James

She sees me as macho, huh? Sure, it's a boost to my ego. Not that I needed it. But coming from her... It feels different.

I'm not immune to the zing of attraction between us, either. It's the fact that she's Phe's friend that stops me from making any overt move on her.

I flick a glance in her direction. She takes a lick of her ice-cream. The sight of her pink tongue sends the blood racing to my groin. My cock stabs against my zipper, wanting out. Heat squeezes my chest. My breathing grows erratic. A few more seconds, and I'll have no choice but to haul her over the center console and across my lap, and—

I push my door open and step out. The cool air washes over me. I take a few cleansing breaths. It somewhat dispels the vanilla and coconut of her scent. Combined with the strawberry and mango of her ice-cream, I was drowning inside.

I walk over to the bin by the side of the road and drop my half-eaten ice cream cup inside. I roll my shoulders, brace myself, and walk back to the Jeep. When I slide back inside, it's to find her watching me with a quizzical expression on her features.

At least, she's finished her ice cream cone. That's something. Unfortunately, her scent of vanilla and coconut engulfs me again. My dick instantly perks up. I ignore it, turn the key in the ignition and move into the road.

"You okay?" she murmurs.

I stay quiet. Yep, I'm taking the easy way out, but fuck that. The faster I get her home, the quicker I can forget that the girl who's haunted my dreams is all grown up, and is now a seductive siren, and move on.

She sighs. "You're back to your TDH stance, I see."

I shouldn't ask her what that means. Likely, it's another ploy to get my attention. Something she seems adept at. "What does TDH mean?" I snap.

"Tall, dark and handsome," she replies, a pleased tone to her words.

Of course, I shouldn't be pleased that she thinks that of me. But I am.

I can't stop myself from sitting even straighter. No more than I can stop my chest from swelling with pride. What a cliché I am. Allowing a woman's admiration to get to me. Not just any woman. *Her* admiration.

How lucky I am to be sitting here, driving my Wrangler, with a beautiful, young woman determined to distract me.

How my fallen teammates would have given anything to be here, instead of me?

How I'd have given my life for them to be alive instead.

I squeeze my fingers around the wheel, bringing my focus back to the present. The last thing I want to do is crash this car with my precious cargo. Once I see her home in one piece, I can go home and get stinking drunk. It's one way of dealing with this remorse I carry around. Survivor's guilt can be a terrible thing. It wrings out your heart and destroys your capacity to feel.

She reaches over and touches the panel on the dash. The music shuts off. I'm grateful for the quiet. Not sure how she knew I needed the silence. But I'm not going to ask.

"You all right?" she asks softly.

I must be losing my touch for keeping my feelings in check, if she could read the emotions my face. I blow out a breath. "I will be."

"Hmm." She looks out the windscreen with interest. "Why don't we get a drink?"

"Eh?" I shoot her a sideways glance.

"Just a drink. No funny business, I promise."

I frown.

"Look, all I have to look forward to is another long day washing dishes in a restaurant tomorrow. I need a night cap to help me sleep."

Despite myself, I'm intrigued. "You work in a restaurant?"

"For my sins." She leans back with a sigh. "I got a scholarship to go to culinary school. Not that it helped. The only job I could find on graduating was as the kitchen porter, aka the dishwasher."

She purses her lips. Her tone is casual but there's frustration behind her words.

"I have a culinary degree. At the very least I should have been able to get a job doing prep for the chefs, but no."

She throws up her hands.

"The London restaurant scene is so competitive. There were so many applicants even for this dishwashing role." She half laughs. "I was lucky I got it. At least, it's a decent restaurant. I should be grateful for that, I suppose."

"You want to be a chef?"

She stares at me.

"What?"

"That's the first complete statement you've spoken to me."

I snort. "No, it's not."

She grins. "No. You're right. But given how you've answered me with grunts, it might as well be."

I can't stop my lips from quirking again. She makes it easy for me to smile. To forget the horrors I've seen. To not spend time mulling over the dangers and the darkness in this world and to focus on the brightness instead. She carries a certain lightness in her that lessens the weight I've carried on my shoulders since my last mission. That is the only reason why I take the next turnoff and head for a nearby bar. A quiet one, this time.

"A whiskey, huh?" She gives me a 'how predictable can you be' look.

Am I getting that formulaic in my life, that a slip of a girl can take one look at me and slot me into a 'type?' The thought is sobering.

The bartender slides a glass of something pink and frothy in her direction. I eye it meaningfully, then her.

She flushes slightly. "Yes, it's a frozen strawberry daiquiri, so?"

"Pot. Kettle." I say mildly.

She raises her glass. "What should we toast to?"

How the fuck am I supposed to know? I stay quiet.

She frowns, then her face brightens. "Oh, I know. Let's toast to getting to know each other."

Something I'm not sure is wise. I worry that the more I get to know her, the more complicated this non-relationship between us will get.

When I don't raise my glass she reaches forward and taps her glass to mine. "Cheers."

I grunt, then take a sip of my whiskey.

She takes a big gulp of her daiquiri and sighs, "I needed that."

"Water is better when you're thirsty." I glance at the bartender, who instantly fills a glass and sets it in front of her.

She stares, first at the bartender, then at me. "How did you do that?"

I frown.

"Get the bartender to do your bidding without talking to him."

I shrug. Then slide the water closer to her. "Drink."

She scowls. "You're bossy."

"Or not." I shrug, then take another sip of my whiskey.

She stares at the water longingly, then lifts the glass to her lips and swallows half of it. She puts it down with a sigh. "Thanks."

I tilt my head.

She wraps her fingers around the stem of her glass. "You're a Marine?"

I stiffen, then nod slowly. It's not something I want to talk about right now. Not when I'm trying to move on from my last mission.

Something in my stance must give away my thoughts, for her voice softens. "I'm sorry, I didn't mean to pry."

"You're not." My voice comes out gritty. I clear my throat. "I don't like talking about what I do when I'm on leave. It's my chance to recharge and put some distance between my job and myself."

"I understand. I don't like talking about how I'm spending all my time washing dishes, after completing a Professional Chef Diploma." As if simply talking about it is traumatic enough, she takes another big gulp of her daiquiri.

"A friend joined the Marines. It seemed like such a heroic thing to do. It spurred me to do the same."

She nods. "I had a childhood friend who insisted she wanted to become a chef. She made me apply to become a chef with her. I got through; she didn't. Suffice to say, our friendship didn't last, but I became a chef."

I swirl the whiskey in my glass. "How long have you known Phe?"

"We met at university. Of course, our disciplines were different. But we became fast friends." She eyes me speculatively, then opens her mouth and shuts it. The struggle to not ask me the question on her mind is real on her face.

I half smile, finding her attempt at granting me my privacy almost endearing. When she flattens her lips and looks like she's about to burst with the effort I sigh. "Go on, ask your question."

A look of relief filters into her features. "Do you enjoy being a Marine?"

"Enjoy?" I twist my lips. "That's not quite the word I'd use."

"Of course. How crass of me. I mean, do you think it's your calling?"

5

Harper

"No, it's not." He tosses back the rest of his whiskey. Follows it up with a few bills. "You done?"

I take in his closed features. The, once again, inscrutable expression on his face and sigh. I shouldn't have asked him the question. But I couldn't help it. Not to mention, he told me to go ahead and ask.

There's something tearing him apart from the inside. And I can't stop until I find out everything about it.

I gulp down the rest of my daiquiri and slip off the barstool. My head spins. "Oops." I giggle and grab at the bar counter.

Instead, my fingers connect with warm skin and hard muscle. I hold on to his arm, and shockwaves sizzle out from the point of contact. The hair on the nape of my neck rises. He looks down from his height, and I tilt my head back to meet his eyes. Those blue eyes of his turns heavier, almost ink-dark with emotion. And I thought this man was emotionless. On the contrary, he's hiding his feelings deep inside.

All it'd take is the right situation... Or the right person... The right woman to unlock whatever it is he prefers to hide.

I sway toward him. A flush stains his cheeks. He lowers his head toward me. Then a glass smashes somewhere in the bar. Both of us jump apart.

"We should get going." He clears his throat.

"Yeah." I swallow, then look away. I snatch my jacket from where it's hanging under the bar counter.

That's the second time this evening we almost kissed. I'd do anything to feel his lips on mine. Unbidden, my gaze falls on his mouth. When he sets his jaw, I raise my gaze to his eyes. Which are, once again, shuttered. He spins around on his heels and walks away. I follow him.

Halfway to the door, a man steps in front of me. He's taller than James. And while he's broader, his muscles seem to be the kind that come from pumping iron at the gym. No doubt, he has tasteless protein shakes for breakfast.

"Excuse me." I try to move around him, but he shifts with me. "Hey, pretty lady, can I buy you a drink?" He leers at me.

Oh, for heaven's sake. Why are men so predictable? "No, thank you." Once more, I try to step past him. Once again, he plants his body in front of me.

"Really?" Anger bubbles low in my belly. "Let me pass."

"Not until you have a drink with me." He reaches out for me.

I step back and brace myself, preparing to knee him in the groin. But suddenly, he's grabbed from behind and shoved to the side, and James stands in front of me.

The other man bellows and charges.

James holds his ground. When the man is close enough, he

shoots out his fist, which connects with the man's cheek. The man sways, then topples over.

"Oh, my god, you knocked him out!" I clap my hands together.

Around us, the people who had frozen burst into action. A couple of well-built men approach us. They are similar enough and dressed in clothes which mirror the man on the ground. Enough to indicate they are my antagonizer's friends.

Without missing a beat, James strikes out again. He catches one of the men under his chin. The man crashes into the table nearby. The people at the table jump up.

He throws another punch which gets the other man in the nose. There's a sound of something breaking.

I wince.

The man screams. Blood erupts from his face. He holds his broken nose and staggers back.

James locks his fingers around my wrist. The next moment, he's dragging me in his wake.

He shoulders past a man, sidesteps another, punches a third, and glares at a fourth, who steps aside.

Adrenaline laces my blood. My pulse rate goes crazy.

I have an impression of fights breaking out around us. Of chairs crashing. Glasses falling to the floor. The scent of alcohol laces the air. It's like I stepped into a scene from a movie. In fact, I've never felt this alive before.

Then we're out the door. The cool air surrounds me. He hauls me to his car, opens the door to the passenger side, and all but throws me inside. Then he's in the driver's seat, pressing down on the accelerator as we drive off.

"Oh my god! Oh my god!" I turn to him. "That was so much fun!"

He shoots me a sideways glance, and whatever he sees on my face has his features softening. "It was, huh?" His lips twitch.

"You bet." I burst out laughing. "The way you took out those men. And did you see how it turned into a full-blown bar fight?" I squeeze my hands together.

"You're one bloodthirsty little thing, aren't you?" He keeps his attention on the road.

"It certainly got the blood flowing." I take in his reddened knuckles. "And got you hurt."

"It'll heal." His tone is dismissive.

"You could come home and let me take care of it." The words are out before I can stop myself. Ugh, that did sound like a blatant invitation, didn't it?

He shoots me a glance that's half amused, half heated. "Did you just invite me to your place?"

"And if I did?" I tip up my chin.

"You're Phe's friend—"

"And you're her older brother. So what? I'm twenty-one. I'm an adult. I can decide for myself who I want to invite home."

He shakes his head. "Oh no, I'm not going to the home of my little sister's best friend."

"Why? Don't you trust yourself?" I flutter my eyelashes at him.

He flashes me another look, from under half-closed eyelashes. "It's you I don't trust."

I scoff. "Why? Do you think I'll throw myself at you?"

"Wouldn't you?"

"I—" I was going to say I wouldn't. But that would be a lie. I'd totally climb this hunk of a man like a tree and cling to him like a koala bear.

"Exactly." He half smiles. When he looks at me again, there's no gloating on his face. Instead, his eyes carry an expression I can only call regretful.

My heart lightens somewhat at that. He does want more, but for some reason, his sense of propriety will not let him take things further with me. He's not only hotter than Hades but he also has a clear sense of right and wrong. Something which endears him even more to me.

The skin around his eyes crinkles. "Why don't I take you to my favorite spot in London instead?"

6

James

"Oh wow… The view is beautiful." She takes in the lights of the city spread out in front of us.

"It certainly is."

Something in my voice makes her turn to look at me, to find I'm looking at her. She flushes deeply. The color stands out on her creamy skin in the moonlight.

We're at the top of Primrose Hill, and London glows beneath the velveteen sky.

I'm entranced by her zest for life. At how she welcomes every experience like it's her first time. Probably because it is. Unlike me. I feel old and jaded. Exhausted by the business of living. Until now, I hadn't realized how burned out I am from my last mission. But meeting her brings home the fact that I've lost my thirst for life.

Somewhere along the way, I stopped believing in the reasons I signed up to be a Marine. Instead, I began to dread the thought of more violence.

Of more teammates being killed or maimed. I've begun to recoil at the prospect of hearing screams of pain. Of smelling burning flesh. Of going into yet another strategy meeting, ordered by the powers that be, where the directives seemed to make no sense.

The sense of idealism and the loyalty to my friend which propelled me to join the Royal Marines has all but faded. I'm carrying out missions based on a sense of duty... Which is not a bad thing, in itself. But it's not enough for me. I need to find what fires me again. I need to find my passion. What lights me up from the inside and makes each day worth living again. I need... To leave the Marines and forge my own path.

The decision which has been hovering at the corners of my subconscious mind crystallizes. I didn't even realize, I've been wanting to make a change in my life. But meeting her precipitated it. I have this gorgeous, utterly entrancing woman to thank for pushing me to arrive at a decision which I have no doubt is going to change the course of my life. The hair on the back of my neck stands up.

My feet seem to move of their own accord.

I reach her, and when I hold out my hand, she places hers in it.

"Thank you."

"For what?" She smiles.

"For being you."

"Oh." She swallows. "That's such a sweet thing to say."

"It's not." I search her features. "It's the truth. Don't ever change, Harper."

She tips up her chin and sways toward me.

It's the most natural thing in the world for me to lower my chin. My lips are poised over hers, her breath warm on my cheek, her green eyes glowing like emeralds, when a dog barks. I blink. *What am I doing?* I step back, let go of her hand.

A dog pads past, tugging at his leash. His owner follows holding a plastic bag in hand.

"James," she whispers.

I shake my head. "Sorry, for a moment there, I forgot myself."

She seems crestfallen. She opens her mouth, then shuts it. Then looks at the view for a few seconds. When she turns back to me, she seems more composed.

"Thanks for bringing me here."

I tilt my head in acknowledgement.

"But the night's not over yet." As if to punctuate her words, her stomach grumbles loudly. "I know this little restaurant which serves the best Italian."

"It's good, right?" She licks her lips.

Instantly, I'm erect. I've grown increasingly hungrier with every mouthful she's eaten. And it's not for food.

A dot of tomato sauce clings to the corner of her mouth. "You have something there," I touch the corner of my lips.

She licks her mouth again, misses it completely.

Without allowing myself to second guess, I reach over and scoop up the sauce. Then I bring it to my mouth and suck on it.

Her pupils dilate. "Umm, why did you do that?"

I survey her features. "I'm not sure," I answer honestly.

She nods slowly. "I'm old enough to know my mind."

For a second there, she does sound wiser than her years. *It doesn't negate the fact that she's my little sister's best friend.* No matter that she's an adult.

"If you were indeed *mature,* you'd know how dangerous it is to hang out with someone like me."

"Someone like you?" She frowns.

"I've seen too much darkness." I look into her eyes. "I've experienced the depths to which humans can fall. I'm so damaged, I'm bound to infect anyone I come in contact with, with my ghosts."

Her features soften. "You may think you're beyond redemption. But from where I am, I see a man who puts his life at stake for his country. Who fights those who'd harm us so I can sleep easy at night. Someone who's noble and dedicated to a cause bigger than himself. The fact that you're hot doesn't hurt either."

She flushes after that last sentence.

Damn, but she's cute. And yes, my ego is more than stoked by her compliments. I try and fail to stop my lips from twitching. "You give me too much credit."

"You face down bullets from enemies in real life, so I don't think I am."

"I have been involved in combat missions." I tilt my head. "But a lot of what I do is strategic. Often, I'm stuck in a room and engaged in intelligence assessments and operational coordination."

"Like I said, you are a real-life hero."

"Thank you." I fork up some of the pasta, chew, then swallow.

"You didn't answer me. How is the food?"

"It's... not bad." I set down my fork.

"Not bad?" She rears back in mock horror. "That's it?"

I tap my fingers on the table. "I can make better pasta than what you get in this restaurant."

"Get out of here," she scoffs.

When I stay silent, genuine amusement filters into her features. "You're not kidding, I take it."

I shake my head slowly. "You and I have a lot more than my sister in common."

It's her turn to set down her cutlery. "Like what?"

"I, too, enjoy cooking."

7

Harper

"No." My jaw drops. Thinking of this man in the kitchen, sleeves rolled up, crafting a dish to satisfy my palate, is the most erotic thing ever.

"Don't look so shocked." He chuckles.

The grumpass who's more given to grunts than words actually chuckles.

His blue eyes turn azure, almost silver. His expression lightens. He seems so much younger than his years.

"I once thought I might pursue a career as a chef. But then"—a shadow crosses his face—"life got in the way."

From wanting to become a chef to becoming a Marine? I wonder what happened to make him change his mind in such a drastic fashion.

He mentioned it was his friend joining the Marines which

inspired him to do the same. But clearly, there's more to that story.

"It's not too late. You can still study to become a chef," I point out.

"It might be a little too late for me," His eyes grow haunted.

"It's never too late." I feel the need to soothe him. To reassure him. To show him that there's more to life than the fatalistic view he seems so keen on taking. "You're what? A decade older than me?"

His forehead furrows. That was a mistake. I shouldn't have brought that up. Clearly, our age gap is an issue for him. But really, what is a decade? "You're in your early thirties. You still have a long life ahead of you."

His lips tighten. "I hope you're right." His voice is somber.

Damn, I'm botching this completely.

He's a Marine. He puts his life on the line every single day, faces death as part of his job, and I just casually threw out "long life ahead of you" like it's a guarantee. Like men in his position don't often come home in flag-draped coffins. It's a reality he lives with. And I had to refer to it in the most tactless fashion.

I mentally shake myself and try again. "What I'm trying to say is, the number of years between us doesn't matter as much as where we are mentally. Our maturity levels. Our life experience."

I mentally shake myself and try again. "Let me try that again. Chronological years don't matter as much as your mental perspective."

He nods slowly. "You're right, of course."

Okay. Good.

His gaze narrows. "But it doesn't negate the fact that you're my little sister's best friend. It's a relationship I don't want to jeopardize."

I frown. "Why would it? Phe's an adult. She doesn't get to dictate who I see or what I do with my personal life. My friendship with her and whatever might happen between you and me are two separate things."

He shakes his head. "They're not separate, Harper. Not when I'm involved. If things go south between us, it puts you in an impossible position. You'd have to choose between your best friend and the guy who hurt you. Or worse, you'd lose her because she'd feel like she has to pick a side. I won't do that to either of you."

I rub at my temple. "I'm really not understanding what you're implying."

His forehead crinkles. He seems to think things through, then sets his jaw as if coming to a decision. "I'm not the relationship kind."

"Okay?" I lower my chin. "I'm twenty-one. I'm not looking for a relationship, either."

"You're looking for something temporary?" The fine wrinkles around his eyes deepen. He doesn't seem happy at the prospect. How strange. I thought he'd find it freeing.

"I'm not looking to marry the first man I sleep with, if that's that you're thinking."

No sooner are the words out than I squeeze my eyes shut. *Damn. Damn. Damn. Did I have to blurt that out?* Color flushes my cheeks. "Can we forget that I said that?" My voice comes out strangled.

When I open my eyes, he's looking at me with shock and something else—*desire?*—in his eyes.

"Oh my god, you like the fact that I haven't slept with anyone?" I whisper.

Also, it's surreal that we're having this conversation so soon after we met. But hey, since it's out in the open, may as well own it.

He rubs the back of his neck, then looks around as if wishing he were elsewhere. "It has a certain appeal," he finally admits.

"But also, it's all the more reason that I'm not going to explore whatever this is between us."

I brace my hands on the table, irritation biting at my chest.

I'm pissed off at myself for being so gauche as to let that slip. But also, I can't believe how quickly he dismissed the connection he feels for me.

"You could go through your entire life and not feel whatever it is that's here between us." I wave my hand in the air.

He considers what I said, then nods. "Perhaps."

"And that doesn't upset you?"

He thinks through my words again. "It does. But my relationship with my sister is just as important."

I throw up my hands. "You're complicating things for no reason."

The skin around his mouth softens. "When you live a little more of life, you'll realize that everything is connected."

"You mean the butterfly effect? I know about that."

"Do you?" He lips twitch.

The humor in his eyes rubs me up the wrong way. "You're not taking me seriously," I snap.

"On the contrary"—his gaze, once more, grows serous—"I find you fascinating. And smart. And gorgeous. And yes, a tad young for me."

His lips twist.

"But your freshness is part of your appeal."

The color of his eyes deepens to midnight. There's no mistaking the intensity of his words. My stomach flips like the contents of a pan which have been set to boil too fast. An electric sensation sizzles across my chest. Being the focus of his attention is like standing too close to an open flame. It's unsettling, dangerous, but impossible to step away from. My breath catches.

"Was that a confession that you find me attractive?" I strive for a lighter tone of voice, but don't quite pull it off.

One side of his lips quirks. "You want me to confirm to you that I also feel this chemistry between us?"

I nod. "It's good to know that whatever I'm feeling is not all one-sided."

"It's not. But I'm also not going to sleep with you. Especially, not now."

He's not saying it's because I'm a virgin, but that's, clearly, a big part of it, too.

The set to his features tells me I can't change his mind. If I belabor the point, it's only going to make him dig in his heels. So, I decide to change track.

I pick up my fork and scoop up more of the pasta, chewing on it thoughtfully.

"What's your favorite dish to cook?"

He accepts the change in subject. "The humble omelet."

"Hmm." I look at him with interest. "Not that humble. It's not easy to make a perfect omelet."

"It's not." His eyes light up with an inner fire. "It's brutally simple yet needs precision and a lightness of touch which only comes with a lot of practice. But even that's not enough. The more you practice the better you get at it, and yet… There's a chance you don't get it right. It's like shooting. You keep at it. You get better with time, but there's always a chance your calculations are off, or the winds change as you shoot, and you miss your mark."

"You're a sniper?" I ask with a flash of insight.

He looks at me with something like admiration. "Royal Marines are commandos first and specialists second. My forte is mission planning and strategy. But yes, I also get sent on high stake missions as a marksman."

I nod slowly. "I can see why both of those would suit your temperament."

"Oh?"

I purse my lips. "I imagine it requires extreme patience and restraint, and likely, an obsession with micro-adjustments. Not to mention, the ability to work under pressure. All of which seem second nature to you."

"We just met, and you think you already know me?" He's not insulted; he's genuinely curious.

"I have good instincts," I say with quiet confidence.

It's something I know about myself. It's why I've kept on this path of becoming a chef, despite the fact that that I have to work my way up from being a dishwasher. Literally. Something in me insists I can do this. Just like I know this man in front of me is going to play a role in my life.

"So do I." He holds my gaze.

The air between us heats. My scalp tingles. I can't get over the fact that, despite his insistence to the contrary, whatever is between us can't be pushed aside. "You can't see a relationship between us. I'm not saying I accept that. But also, I'm not going to try to change your mind."

He narrows his gaze. "So, what are you hinting at?"

I tighten my hold on my fork, then peek up at him from under my eyelashes, "You could give me this one night?"

8

James

"We'd spend it talking and exploring this city. All very innocent." Her eyes are wide, her expression is innocent. She's anything but. She's a siren who could easily seduce me.

When I stay silent, she tosses her head. "Don't tell me you don't trust yourself around me?'

I don't, but I'm not going to admit that aloud. I'm also not immune to the light of challenge in her eyes. My ego won't let me back down from it. So, I nod. "Fine. We'll talk. And then I'll take you to my favorite breakfast spot."

She glances at her watch. "Huh, didn't realize it's already two a.m."

I haven't noticed the hours passing either. And I haven't thought about my past or my last mission—when I'd barely managed to escape with my life—during the time I've been with her. I wouldn't have thought this slip of a girl could distract me enough that I'd finally escape the voices in my head which have haunted me.

I lean back in my seat. "So, where do you want to go?"

"I grew up in Yorkshire, so I'm still discovering this city." She taps her finger against her cheek, a considering look on her face. "Why don't you surprise me?"

The light of challenge in her eyes blazes brighter, and something primal inside me roars to life. My heart slams against my ribs like it's trying to break free. My spirit feels untethered, weightless, like I've been drowning for years and suddenly remembered how to breathe.

I feel more alive than I have since before the blood and darkness tried to hollow me out. It's what propels me to my feet, drawn to her like gravity, like inevitability.

I allow myself a small smile, knowing it's probably a mistake. "Come on, then."

"I've never been on Waterloo Bridge when there were no people on it." She looks out on the London skyline. The Tower Bridge, The Shard, The Gherkin, and the Walkie-Talkie building are all lit up. The city feels endless but also, intimate.

"Me neither," I say in a hushed tone.

It's not like anyone can hear us. And yet, it feels right to lower my tone, in keeping with the silence surrounding us. A lone boat heads toward the bridge, then passes under us.

She turns to face me, her back to the bridge. "You do this often? Spend the night talking with women you've only just met?"

I allow myself a small smile. "No, I don't. You're the first, and you know that."

When I look at her, she' s smiling too. "Just wanted to hear you say it."

I chuckle.

Her smile fades a little. She scans my features, seemingly transfixed by whatever she sees.

"What?" I arch an eyebrow.

"You look different when you smile. The weight of your worries seems to fall away. And you seem almost…approachable."

"Thanks?" I drawl.

"Of course, the forbidding, dark, smoldering looks also add to your appeal."

"Smoldering?" I bark out a laugh.

Yeah, I've never laughed as much as I have with her. She's dangerous. I should put distance between us. But…for the first time in a long time, I'm having so much fun. And I do feel so much lighter. Enough that I want to, at least, allow myself this night. I want to create memories to last me through my last tour. I stiffen.

When did I made up my mind that I'm leaving the Marines?

I took time off to decide what I want to do with my future. And meeting her distracted me from my immediate concerns, giving me perspective. Enough that my subconscious mind decided my path of action.

"Definitely smoldering." She grins up at me. "It's probably going to boost your already ginormous ego when I tell you, you're the most striking, most charismatic, most masculine man I've ever met, but there you go."

A gust of wind blows a strand of hair across her forehead. Without giving myself time to second guess myself, I reach over and tuck it behind her ear.

The slide of her silky soft hair against my skin feels decadent. Like diving headfirst into a pool filled with chocolate and cream, and now, I'm sinking fast. The temptation to keep my hand on her, to pull the band from her hair, then bury my nose in her lustrous locks is overwhelming.

The ardor of my longing hits me with such force that it brings me back into my body.

I step back. Then, to stop myself from doing something I'll regret, like kiss her, I stuff my hands in my pocket. "I'm not criticizing your perceptions of me. But—" I roll my shoulders back. "You haven't seen enough of the world to draw that conclusion."

She firms her lips. "I'm not saying you're wrong. But also, there's something called instinct. And mine insists, you're one of a kind."

Her eyes shine up at me with something close to hero-worship. A part of me revels in it. I'd love to be her hero. To take her away from her currently dreary job and into a life where I can take care of her. Only, she's too young. And I wouldn't be able to guarantee her forever. Or even a short-term relationship, for that matter. If I told her that, she'd insist she'd be fine with it. But I know, she'd eventually want more. And I wouldn't be able to give it to her. But then, the thought of being her first... Fuck. That's too much responsibility for me, at this stage.

"Oh no—" She shakes her head. "No. No. No. Whatever it is you're thinking, you need to stop it right now."

I almost chuckle at that. "You have no idea what I'm thinking."

She scoffs. "I bet it's the same ol', same ol', thoughts of protecting me and walking away from me for all the reasons we've spent the night discussing."

I look away from her at the lights in the distance, then back at her. "What you don't know is that beneath all that is this overwhelming desire to carry you out of here and to my bed and have my way with you, until you can't walk for days."

"Oh—" She freezes with her mouth open, her eyes wide. Except for the wind which rustles the tips of her hair, she might as well be a frozen tableau. Her surprise, combined with the blush that stains her cheeks, is a thing of beauty.

I reach over and push up against her chin, so she closes her lips. "Oh my god." She swallows. "That was...hot."

Her eyes gleam.

"Also, if you were hoping to put me off by declaring your intentions, it's had the opposite effect."

I shake my head. "You don't want to see the ugliness I have in me. Or touch the damage that's changed me forever. I don't travel light. I carry too many ghosts."

She closes the distance to me, until the tips of her shoes brush mine. Her green eyes shine like dew on spring grass. Her lips part. She's danger wrapped in beauty. A promise I can't trust myself to keep. I'd hurt her. I'd destroy her faith in romance and splinter the stars in her eyes. And yet, I can't make myself step away. Not when she goes up on tiptoe and raises her chin. Not when she wraps her hand around my neck and urges me to dip my head.

I allow her to pull me down halfway to her lips, then stop, my gaze fixed firmly on her plump mouth. My heart swelling in my chest until I'm sure it's going to break through my ribcage.

She tries to pull me down further, but I don't give in.

Her lips turn down. "You're stubborn."

"I am."

"And pig-headed."

"I've been called worse."

She licks her lips. The blood drains to my groin.

She jumps up, still unable to brush her lips against mine, and makes a sound of frustration. "So not fair that you're so much taller than me." She pouts.

Those luscious lips form a moue which plays havoc with my

blood pressure. My pulse rate shoots up. She's so damn sexy. And tempting. And seductive. One taste. Just one taste… How would that feel?

She huffs, then begins to move back.

That's when I lower my head and capture her mouth with mine.

9

Harper

Ohmigod. Oh my god. *Oh. My. God.* He's kissing me.

James Hamilton is kissing me.

My best friend's very hot, very sexy, very alpha older brother is kissing me.

I part my lips. He makes a rumble of approval in his chest. Then he slides his tongue over mine and I. Am. Lost. Sinking. Spinning.

He deepens the kiss, and I feel it all the way through my toes. It's as if he's sucking my very spirit out. My heart skips a beat. The very core of my being flutters.

I close my eyes and kiss him back deeply, savoring the softness of his tongue, the hardness of his lips, the heat of his body surrounding mine, cocooning me, and at the same time, turning me on. And then, I'm free. So quickly, I stumble back. He rights me with a touch on my shoulder. I feel the reverberations echo through my body. Then he releases me. Steps back.

I look up into his stunning face, feeling like I've stumbled onto something magical and beautiful and earth-shattering and everything I've ever imagined but didn't think possible.

"Wow," I manage to whisper.

He doesn't reply. His brows knit. His gorgeous lips tighten. He scrutinizes my face like I'm a puzzle he can't solve. Whatever he sees there deepens the furrow between his eyebrows. He takes another step back, taking the heat with him.

I'm suddenly cold. Bereft. I shiver.

He slips his coat off and places it around my shoulders. His gesture feels intimate. But his gaze has turned impersonal. Whatever emotions I glimpsed earlier have been replaced by wariness.

"You felt it too, didn't you?"

He stays silent.

"That kiss wasn't one-sided. I know, it moved you as much as me."

His lips tighten.

"So why are you putting distance between us? Is it because you're scared about what it made you feel?"

Something shifts behind his eyes. "I am scared," he admits.

"Oh." I blink. Did not expect him to acknowledge that.

"And you're right, that kiss felt different. It moved something in me. In fact"—his forehead furrows—"it reminded me that I'm not ready for a relationship."

"I'm not looking for a relationship," I burst out.

He lowers his chin. "That might be the case. Now. But in my experience, at some point, you'd expect more of me, and I wouldn't be able to give you that."

I stare at him, frustrated. "Are you trying to tell me I don't know my mind?"

His features soften. "Of course, not. I'm trying to protect you from getting hurt."

"Shouldn't I get to make that choice?" I tuck my elbows into my sides. This is such a ridiculous conversation. I want to be with him. And he thinks he's going to stop me from getting hurt by turning me down.

"Of course, you should be the one to decide what's right for you. But in this case, you should trust me when I say that you don't want to be with me."

"But what if I do want to be with you?" Argh, I hear my words, and my cheeks heat. I want to tell him that I'd choose to be with him, even if it's only for a few hours. That I'd walk away after. But I already know that's a lie. Once I've been with James, I won't want anyone else. He'll spoil me for any other man. But oh, how amazing it would feel to be with him. Some of my feelings must show on my face, for the blue of his eyes deepens. A nerve throbs at his temple. The chemistry between us spikes.

"Damn, woman you're making this really difficult." He swallows. "But I promise you, I'm not the kind of man you want to be with. I'm not good for you, Harper."

Hearing my name from his mouth sends shiver down my spine. My nipples tighten. My scalp tingles. I sway toward him. He cups my cheek and lowers his head. I close my eyes, tip up my chin, and feel the warmth of his breath on my cheek, on my lips.

Then just like that, it's gone. And so is his touch.

I snap my eyes open, to find him looking at me with a tortured expression in his eyes. "I can't, Harper. I can't let you spoil your life. You're young. You have much to accomplish. You don't need someone as jaded and cynical as me. Someone with ghosts from the past which haunt me and hold me back, someone who's seen things no man should and still be alive, someone who'd taint your innocence, someone who'd drag you down into the darkness with him. I'm not the man for you."

"But what if you were?" I swallow. "What if you were the man I was waiting for."

His lips twist. A sadness filters into his eyes. "I'm not."

"How can you say that with so much confidence?"

"Because you haven't seen enough of the world yet to know what you want."

I nod slowly. "What you're saying is true. But if that kiss was any indication, I know it's going to be amazing with you."

"And I'd be your first. I admit, that thought makes me want to throw you over my shoulder and carry you off to my bed and ravish you, but I'm not selfish enough to do that."

"What do you mean?"

"You'd catch feelings. And I wouldn't be able to give you what you wanted."

"You mean, I'd want more than sex?'

He nods. "And I don't want a relationship right now. I'd break your heart. And my sister would hate me for it."

I grit my teeth. There's a lot of truth to what he's saying. But that doesn't make it easier for me to accept it. I open my mouth to protest, but he holds up his hand. "Please. I've made up my mind. This... Whatever it is—is over. I shouldn't have agreed to spend the last few hours with you. It's time I take you home."

10

James

"So, this is it?" She stares straight ahead through the windshield of the car.

I drove her home through the silent streets of the city, hoping to prolong the time I had with her.

But it's just four a.m. The streets are hushed. Any scattered traffic has melted away. It's that hour when even insomniacs finally fall asleep. It's as if the entire city is holding its breath. Which is the only reason my chest felt too tight.

I made it to her address in less than half the time it'd normally take me. And cursed the fact that I couldn't find any further excuse to spend more time with her.

I parked in front of her apartment block, and neither of us moved for a few seconds. Then I unlocked the car doors. That broke the silence.

She turns to me. "You sure you don't want to come in?"

I half smile. "Nice try, but no."

She sighs. "You're obstinate."

"And you're beautiful."

She flushes. "You shouldn't say things like that, especially when you've made it clear, you don't want anything to do with me."

I frown. The hurt in her voice twists my guts and settles uncomfortably in my belly.

"You understand why though, don't you?"

"Because of your misplaced sense of responsibility?"

My lips twitch. How I love her feistiness. The way she doesn't back down. How she doesn't hesitate to speak her mind, holds her ground without flinching. How she screws up her eyes when she smiles. The sense of wonder on her face when I showed her my favorite part of the city. How her green eyes shine like emeralds when she's turned on, how she blushes prettily.

She's the most beautiful woman in the world. And no one can come close to her.

I'll never forget her. And I'm walking away from her. I set my jaw. I *will* walk away from her. I have to. It's what's best for both of us.

I'm not in the right frame of mind to have someone in my life. And she… She's just starting her's.

"Because it's the right thing to do," I murmur.

Her lips turn down. "Didn't think you'd turn out to be this decent."

"Oh, I'm not." I squeeze my fingers around the steering wheel to stop myself from reaching for her. "But on this occasion… It's too important."

Her chest rises and falls. Her chin trembles. Then she gives a firm nod and composes herself. "Right then." She holds out a hand.

I glance at it, then back at her face.

She sees the determination on my features, and her jaw drops. "Not even a handshake?"

"Not even a handshake." Because if I touch her, I will not let her go. And I can't do that. I push my door open, step around the car, and hold her door open. She lowers her feet to the ground. I shut the door behind her, walk her to the entrance of the building. She keys in a code, and the door unlocks. She pushes the door open, turns to face me. "Thanks for walking me to my doorstep."

"You're welcome." I tilt my head. "If things had been different—"

"But they're not." She swallows. "Goodbye, James."

She steps back. The door slams shut. I stand there, staring at the wood. Fucking hell. What have I done. The most beautiful thing in my life, and I let her go.

I did the right thing.

I can't mess up the relationship with my sister.

And I would have, if I'd slept with Harper.

Maybe in another time. In another place. Maybe at some point in the future our paths will cross again?

Maybe.

I stay there for a few seconds more, then turn and walk to the car. As if in a trance, I start the engine and ease the vehicle forward. I'm not sure how I make the ride home, but once I'm in my penthouse, I pour myself a whiskey. Then stand on the balcony and take in the lights of the city. It reminds me of how she gasped on seeing the cityscape from Primrose Hill.

And how I'll never again see the skyline of the city without remembering her.

I'll never forget her.

My phone buzzes. I pull it out of my pocket. It's from my commanding officer, so I answer it. "Hamilton."

"I know you're on leave, but there's a developing situation, and I need you on it."

I toss back the rest of my whiskey. "How soon, Sir?"

"Wheels up tomorrow at oh-nine-hundred hours."

I roll my shoulders back. "I'll be there, Sir. But you should know, this will be my last mission."

To find out what happens next read The Unwilling Bride by L. Steele, James and Harper's story.

Download it from the QR code

How to get your physical copy in 60 seconds:

1 **Open your camera:** Point your phone's camera at the QR code as if you're taking a photo.

2 **Tap the link:** A link will pop up on your screen. Tap it to land directly on the book's Amazon page.

3 **Select "Paperback":** Before you hit buy, make sure the **Paperback** format is selected (it's the one that feels best in your hands).

4 **One-Click Buy:** Tap "**Buy now**" to send a fresh copy to your doorstep.

5 **Check your mail:** Keep an eye on your porch! Your new escape is officially en route and will be waiting for you in just a few days.

6 **Happy reading:** Get cozy, crack the spine, and enjoy that

"new book" smell. (And maybe set an alarm, because "just one more chapter" is a dangerous game). 📖

Here's an excerpt from The Unwanted Wife by L. Steele, Skylar & Nathan's story.

Skylar

"I can't do this." I lock my fingers together and narrow my gaze at my reflection. I'm in the tiny bathroom adjoining my office at the back of my bakery—my baby, my enterprise into which I've poured my life savings. And now, it's going to shut down. Unless I find the money for the rent next month... And for the utilities to keep the lights on so the sign on the shopfront continues to be lit up in pink and yellow neon... And for the supplies I need to continue baking. *The Fearless Kitten* is more than my dream; it's my whole life. What I've worked toward since I was sixteen and knew I was going to become the most phenomenal baker in the world. And now, I'm going to lose it.

"Sure, you can do it." My brother encourages me from the doorway. "You can do anything you set your mind to."

"That's what I used to think. It's why I started this pastry shop." I was twelve when I discovered I was good at baking. That, combined with my love for desserts, meant I knew what I wanted to do with my life.

Two years ago, I moved to London to work at a well-known patisserie. I began scouting for a location for my place while I saved every single penny I could.

A year ago, I found the perfect place, and my little artisan bakery with coffee shop seating was born. Of course, I work eighteen-hour workdays, which means I have almost no social life. I barely manage a few hours of sleep in my little apartment over the shop. But nothing can dampen my spirits. I'm spending my days churning out cakes and pastries. It's what I've dreamed of for so long. Only issue?

I don't have the money to advertise, and despite having a social media post go viral—which is when a lot of people look at your social media feed—and result in a surge of customers, I'm not making enough to salvage my business.

"Don't give up. You have to believe this can take off." Ben's voice is confident. If only I shared his optimism.

"Oh, trust me, I want to believe. But blind faith in yourself only takes you so far." I wish I could do better at spreading the word about the place and bringing in new customers. I seem to suck at everything outside of baking. It's why my business is on the decline.

"Success is what's beyond the dark night of the soul," my brother, ever the wise one, remarks.

"Is that a saying among you Royal Marines?" I scoff.

"It's—"

The bell over the door at the front of the shop tinkles.

"—your destiny." His lips curve in a smile.

"What?" I blink.

"The bell—it's your future calling."

I roll my eyes. "If you say so."

"Go on, your customer is waiting." My brother walks over and kisses my forehead. "Good luck. Remember, when one door closes, another one opens. Or the one I prefer, she who leaves a trail of glitter is never forgotten."

"Eh?" I stare. "What does that have to do with my situation?"

"Nothing, but it did cheer you up."

I roll my eyes, then can't stop myself from chuckling.

"That's my girl." He pats my shoulder.

Yep, that's my brother. The ever-cheerful, never-surrender person. "You'll see; it will work out." He turns me around and points me in the direction of the doorway leading to the shop. "Go on now."

"Whatever you say, big bro."

I was ten when my father passed, and Ben became the de facto father figure in my life. I'm fifteen years younger than him, an "oops baby," born when my mother was in her early forties. I hero-worshipped Ben, who, in turn, took care of me and never let me feel the loss of my father. And when my mother passed away, he took a leave of absence and came home and stayed with me, until he was assured I was ready to pick myself up and move on. He's the most important person in the world, in my life, in so many ways. And the fact that he fights wars so I can be safe is a source of the utmost pride for me. It's one of the reasons I feel terrible about being on the verge of bankruptcy. I want Ben to be proud of me.

"This is my last chance to get things right. If I can't find a way to pay off my debts, I'll have no choice but to shut down." I hear my words and realize I'm being negative. The exact opposite of my brother. I expect him to tell me off, but there's no answer. I turn to find he's left the shop. Not that I blame him. He has a two-week break before he has to ship out again. I suspect he's gone to meet his current squeeze. Ben never lacks female companionship.

As for me? I need to face whatever's in my destiny. If only my every decision didn't impact Hugo. If only I weren't running out of money to keep him in the care home that provides round-the-clock attention for him. If I can't pay next month's fees—no, I'm not going there. I will not contemplate the repercussions of what would happen if I didn't come up with the money, and fast.

With a last tug at the neckline of my blouse, which dips a little too low in the front, and which I wore to try and cheer myself up—big fail, there—I march out of the kitchen and go behind the counter. And all the air whooshes out of my lungs.

The man standing in the middle of the bakery is so big, he

seems to occupy all of the space in my little bakery. He's so tall, I have to tilt my head back to meet his gaze. And his shoulders—those shoulders I once held onto—are wider than I remember. They're broad enough to block out the view of the rest of the space.

His biceps stretch the sleeves of his suit, which must cost my entire annual rent to buy, given its tailor-made finish. He's wearing a black silk tie, and his jacket is black. Wait, a suit? I've never seen him in a suit before, but OMG, does he do it justice. I take in that lean waist, and those massive thighs, which seem ready to burst the seams of his pants, and between them, the tent that was the object of my obsession for so long. He prowls over to the counter and whoa, that predatory walk of his, the way he seems to glide across the floor with the gait of a barely tamed animal turns my bones to jelly.

"There was no one at the counter when I walked in. No wonder, you need a cash infusion," a familiar voice growls.

What the—? How dare he say that! I wrench my gaze up to his face. And any remaining thoughts in my head drain away. I was prepared to give him a piece of my mind, but all of the pieces have scattered.

Those eyes—one piercing blue, the other an amber brown. Those heterochromatic eyes, which have always had the effect of reducing me to a mindless blob of need, stare into mine.

My entire body hurts. My shoulder muscles turn into cement blocks. My stomach twists. It feels like I've run into a wall. Frissons of shock reverberate down my spine, and when he rakes his gaze down to my chest, his entire body seems to tense. He brings his gaze back to my face, and it feels like I've been punched in the gut. Again.

"What are you doing here?" I manage to croak around the ball of emotion in my throat.

"What do you think I'm doing here?" His jaw tics, a muscle

spasms in his jaw, and he curls his fingers into his sides. There's so much tension radiating from him, I feel faint. Apparently, he doesn't like what he sees.

That makes two of us. Nathan-bloody-Davenport. My brother's best friend. The man I've had a crush on for more than half my life. The man who turned me down when I threw myself at him the day of my eighteenth birthday party. Not before he kissed me, though.

He hauled me to him, thrust his tongue between my lips, and ravaged my mouth. He squeezed my ample butt and drew me against him, and I felt every inch of what he was packing. The kiss seemed to go on and on. My head spun. My knees gave way underneath me. I stumbled, and he straightened me. Only to tear his mouth from mine and stare into my face, his chest heaving, his breath coming in gusts that seemed to swell his shoulders. He raked his gaze across my features, like he was seeing me for the first time. Like he wanted to throw me down and mount me right there.

"Nate…" I breathed his name.

"Starling," he whispered against my lips. The sound of his voice seemed to cut through his reverie, for the next second, he released me and jumped back.

A look of confusion, then regret, then anger swept over his features. I felt his rejection even before he blanked all expression from his face. "I'm sorry, I shouldn't have done that, Skye." He turned on his heel and walked out of my birthday celebration, and our house. And my life.

That was it; he cut off all communication with me. I never saw him again. Over the last five years, I've heard about his progress in the Marines from my brother, but I never set eyes on him. Until today.

"You're the last person I want to speak to." I cross my arms over my chest, thereby pushing my breasts up higher. His eyes move down before he forces them back to my face. *It's not that I want to flaunt my double-D tits. Okay, okay, maybe I do. Maybe, I want to make him realize what he's been missing.* I'm proud of my assets. I might be a size sixteen, but I've never tried to conceal my full figure. So what if I want to run and hide right now?

"The feeling's mutual," he growls.

And the sound is so freakin' hot, so caveman like, my ovaries seem to quiver. Just because my body can't control itself doesn't mean I find him attractive. Nope, it doesn't mean anything that I haven't stopped thinking of him all these years.

I draw myself up to my full height. Not that it helps, considering I'm five-feet four-inches tall, and he's a good foot taller than me. Still, this is my space. "This is my shop, and you need to leave."

"Trust me, I wouldn't be here if I had any other option," he sneers.

"What's that supposed to mean?"

"You're looking for a bailout."

"Excuse me?" I gape at him.

"Your business is in trouble. You need money to pay off your debts."

My flush intensifies. Heat crawls up my cheeks, all the way to the roots of hair, followed closely by anger. *How dare he walk in and throw my failure in my face? How dare he not talk to me all these years, only to reappear at the worst possible moment? And right after my brother told me it was my destiny come-a-calling when the bell to the shop rang.*

"Wait, did Ben put you up this?"

"Eh?" He stares at my lips. His gaze is so intent that the frisson of awareness, which has crackled up my spine since he arrived, flares into a full-blown shiver. I shake my head, ignoring the buzz of electricity that has always hummed between us. "Are you here because Ben asked you to help me out?"

A weird look comes into his eyes. He shifts his weight from foot to foot. "I'm here because my grandfather is the chairman of the Davenport Group of companies, and he thinks your bakery would make for a good investment."

"He does?"

"I'm yet to be convinced." He crosses his arms across his chest.

So that's how it's gonna be, eh?

He glances toward the counter, taking in the various desserts on display, and his frown deepens. I follow his gaze and take in the tray of cupcakes displayed: Sp1cy Scene, Red Room, Velvet Ties, Purple Patches, Cave Wonder, The Vanilla Vajayjay, The Earth Moved… You have to admit, they're innovative names for the treats.

I named the first one in jest, but it proved to be a hot topic of discussion among fellow spicy book readers like me. Before I knew it, I'd ended up naming many of my desserts in a similar vein.

In fact, the dessert shaped like the backside of a woman and called Spanked is one that customers seem to love. Then there's my other hit, a chocolate cake shaped like a vibrator and called C!itasaurus. Yep, they love that one. Also, another raspberry-infused one in the shape of a peach called Moist Goodness, not to forget the honey-glazed fruit cake in the form of a beehive called the Honey Pot, and the strawberry and cream-topped, fig-shaped shortbread I named Sweet Bits. Finally, the doughnut-shaped dark chocolate glazed treat called—you guessed it—A1phah0le, which readers love when I cater at book events.

You'd think business is booming, and I certainly have my share of loyal customers, but it's not enough to keep me in the black. I need to bring in new customers, and a lot more of them.

He stabs his forefinger at the display. "Is this a joke?"

Skylar

A-n-d that was the absolutely wrong thing to say. No one insults my baby—my bakery, my dream—and gets away unscathed.

"I can assure you; they are popular amongst my customers."

He turns those searing eyes on me, and it feels like I'm looking into the depths of a frozen lake. The surface seems able to bear my weight, but one wrong step, and I'm going to fall right through and find myself trapped. I try to breathe, but all of the oxygen in the room has been sucked out by his presence. My pulse crashes in my ears, and my nerve endings are so tightly stretched, I fear they'll snap any second. And when he shoves a hand in his pocket, pulling the fabric of his pants taut over that bulge between his legs, a slow thud flares to life between mine.

I *cannot* find him attractive. Cannot risk acknowledging this chemistry that thickens the air between us. Not when I need his help to save my business. Not when I know who he is, and he's definitely out-of-bounds. Forbidden. Sirens go off in my mind. *Back away. It's not worth taking on the humungous backlog of complications that are going to come with having anything to do with him.*

Then a look of boredom crosses his face. He yawns, and my pulse rate shoots up.

Strike out everything I felt earlier. It's definitely worth taking on every challenge that comes with getting him to cough up money, because by God, he needs to realize the world doesn't revolve around him. How can anyone be this full of himself? This insensitive?

Anger squeezes my chest. Adrenaline laces my blood. *And how dare he turn the most important meeting of my life into... into... something that doesn't merit even a few seconds of his attention?*

"I've seen everything I need to see. Goodbye." He turns to leave.

What the—? He's leaving? Does that mean he's decided against investing in the bakery? Think! You need to say something to stop him. You cannot afford to piss off the one guy who might be able to help save your bakery.

"Wait, don't you want to taste my wares?" I burst out.

He freezes mid-step. His shoulders seem to swell. The planes of his back rise and fall, and the jacket pulls even tighter. *Is he going to burst out of his skin and go all Hulk on me?* I swallow. And when he turns slowly and makes a growling sound at the back of his throat, I have to stop the yelp that almost spills from my mouth. Every single cell in my body has woken up and is doing the hula. *Stop that. You can't feel this drawn to this... To this arrogant beast who rejected you.*

But I also need his help. I have to save my business from going bust. And if that means swallowing my pride, then so be it. I tip up my chin and straighten my back. "I... I mean, maybe you want to taste my Honey Pot?" *Ugh. Didn't mean it to come out like that.*

His left eyelid, the one covering his blue eye, twitches, and he seems one step closer to either having a breakdown or walking away. Neither of which is desirable.

"Oh, *Fraggle Rock*. What I meant to say is, you'll definitely like the Purple Patches." I point to the range of cupcakes showcased under the counter.

"Did you use *Fraggle Rock* as a swear word?" He stares.

"I did. It's because my mother hated me swearing—being a girl, and all that." I roll my eyes. That condition had *not* applied to my brother. "So instead, I began to use names of TV series as swear words. Also, you could try the C!itasaurus?" I look at him hopefully.

"The whatasaurus?" He tilts his head. His gaze is, once again, fixed on my mouth. My thighs clench, and moisture laces the flesh between my legs. I push away the burst of awareness which seems to have stuck its claws into my skin. No way am I going to succumb to his magnetism, which has multiplied in the years since I last saw him. Especially not when his jerkhole factor hasn't reduced, either.

It's always been a mystery to me why I found his arrogance

such a turn on. Now, I'm also reminded of how he always managed to get on my nerves. Not that it stopped me from throwing myself at him. A mistake I'm not going to make again. When I named that cupcake, it seemed like a stroke of genius. Having to pronounce it aloud in front of the Hulk, however, negates any laughs I've had about it so far.

"Uh, you know what I mean?" The color of my cheeks deepens and spreads to my chest. My entire body seems like it's on fire.

"No, I don't," he says in a low, hard voice.

I shiver. "You know that…that…pink pastry between the blue cakes that looks like…" I glance around, then slide open the glass door to the under-counter area. I pull on a pair of disposable gloves, reach in and, instead of the C!itasaurus, slide one of the fig-shaped desserts onto a plate. I place it on the counter. "Actually, I think you should eat my Moist Goodness, and everything will be clear to you, and—"

I hear a gnashing sound, and when I dare to peek at Mr. Grouchy Face, I see the muscles of his jaw ripple. *Oh no, at this rate, he's going to crack a molar. Or two.*

I blink rapidly. "Maybe we should start afresh?"

"Start afresh?" he asks in a tone that implies he'd rather have never met me.

Yeah, me, too. Unfortunately, I don't have that luxury. "You know, pretend we don't know each other. Pretend the last few minutes never happened?" *Pretend that kiss is not seared into my brain, and into other parts of my body I'm not going to think about.*

I pull off my gloves and hold out my hand. "Skylar Potter." Then, because I hate my life and because, apparently, the connection between my brain and my mouth has been lost under the force of his glower, I smile. "No relation to Harry, as you're aware."

"Harry?" He looks at my slim, pink-tipped fingers, then back at my face, and makes no move to shake my hand.

I set my jaw. *Oh, my god, he's so rude, I should slap one of the pies baking in my oven into his face. Only, they're too good to waste. Also, I can't risk messing up a pie when I need every sale I can get.* Every part of me wants to turn and run out of here. But I can't. I owe it to myself, to my dream, to give this one last shot. *I will not give up easily. I will not. I will stay polite, even if it kills me.* I manage to bare my teeth in the resemblance of a smile. "You know, Harry Potter? Boy wizard? *Evanesco.*" I pretend to flick my wand in his direction.

His jaw hardens further.

Ooh, he looks pissed. The tips of his ears have turned white. Also, the end of his nose. Also, the vanishing spell on him didn't work. His Royal Dickness is still here, larger than life and glowering at me.

"I'm sooo immersed in the Potterverse. Oh, and Taylor Swift. I love Taylor Swift." I beam at him.

His frown deepens.

"I'm guessing you're not a Swiftie?" I nod.

"What's that?" he asks in a contemptuous tone.

"Those of us who love Taylor Swift call ourselves Swifties."

"Sounds contagious," he sneers.

I ignore his cantankerous attitude because I need to charm him. And because I desperately need him to fork over the money I need. "I love her songs, don't you?" I chirrup.

His fingers curl into fists at his sides. Which is not a good sign. Then, because I love to go from the sublime to the surreal, I smile even wider. "Guess which Hogwarts' house Taylor Swift belongs to?" I toss my hair over my shoulder.

"Hogwhat?" He seems like he's about to have a cardiac event. Or like he went to sleep and woke up in an alternate reality. This is bad. So bad.

And I have to go and put my foot in it by prompting him, "Hogwarts."

"Hogwhat?" he snaps again.

This time, the light goes on in my brain. "Oh, you haven't heard of Hogwarts?" I titter. "That's okay. I wasn't alive when *Titanic* hit the cinemas, either..." *Don't say it, don't say it.* "Unlike you."

He blinks slowly.

"I meant the movie, not the actual event when the Titanic hit an iceberg and sank."

His jaw tics.

"Not that you were alive when the Titanic sank." I cough. "Even *I* know you're not *that* ancient."

A nerve pops at his temple. That's not a good sign, is it? *Zip your lips. Just shut up already.*

"Not that I'm implying you're old or anything." I try to contain my laughter and end up snorting—ugh, bad habit. "The grey in your hair adds to your distinguished appearance. Besides, you're only fifteen years older than me." *Oh no, I don't think that makes it better.*

The veins on his throat stand out in relief. I try to swallow, but my throat is so dry, it feels like sharp knives line my gullet. I flick out a tongue to wet my lips, and his eyes gleam. He watches my mouth with a rapacious gaze. Every part of his body seems to have turned to stone. Watching me with such intensity, he seems to have turned into a predator who's planning every possible way to jump me. If he had a tail, I think it'd be swishing from side to side.

The silence deepens. It doesn't stop me from shaking a finger at him. "You, mister, need a crash course in pop culture. Although, I suppose, I shouldn't expect someone who has grey at his temples to have a sense of the zeitgeist."

"The fuck you prattling on about?" he bites out through gritted teeth.

"Whoa, hold on, no need to show me your horns." *Although, I'd love to see the one between your legs.* "In fact, you look so angry, I'm expecting you to breathe fire at any moment." *You can turn into a dragon and carry me away anytime.* "And seriously, you should taste this." I push the plate with the moist, pink-and-white, fig-shaped shortbread in his direction. It has a button between the lips made of edible silver leaf and there's glitter around it.

"My desserts are awesome; one bite, and you'll be a convert." I nod.

He stares.

"Unless you're worried you'll get addicted to my Sweet Bits." I tip up my chin.

Did I say *my* sweet bits? I did say *my* sweet bits. "I meant the dessert that I've named Sweet Bits, not *my* sweet bits." I hear my words, and argh, didn't mean for them to sound so… provocative. But I'm not going to apologize for that. Hell no.

"Well? You going to taste it or what?" I scowl.

He must see the challenge in my eyes and, alpha male that he is, of course, he doesn't back down. Without taking his gaze off of my face, he licks the cream from the hollow in the center. A thousand little fires flare to life under my skin. I swallow; my breath grows shallow. He bites down on one of the plump lips, and a shiver grips me. I clutch at the edge of the counter. The pulse at the base of my throat speeds up. And when he pops the other lip into his mouth, I gulp. He brings his thumb and fore-finger to his mouth and sucks on them, and a breathy moan leaves my lips.

"Not bad." He shrugs.

I stare. "What do you mean, *not bad?! That* is my best-seller."

"It was okay." He looks down his nose from his superior height. "I admit, the names you give your baked goods are creative, but I'm not sure that's enough for me to approve the takeover."

"Takeover?" I stiffen. "Who's talking about a takeover?"

"It's the only way I'd consider investing in your business."

"I only need help," I say through gritted teeth.

"That's putting it mildly. I reached out to the bank you took the loan from—"

"You reached out to my bank?" I burst out.

"You don't think I'd be here without due diligence—"

I cut in, "The terms of my deal with them are confidential." I lock my fingers together.

"Not when you're about to go bankrupt. When they realized the Davenport Group was considering an acquisition—"

"An investment; a loan; that's *all* I'm looking for. Something to tide me over and buy me some time until I get back on my feet."

"Keep fooling yourself. You might be a good baker—"

"So you did like my dessert," I declare in a triumphant voice.

"—but you're not a businessperson, by any stretch of the imagination."

Oh, my god! What I wouldn't give to wipe that smug look off his face.

"There are ups and downs in any business." I lock my fingers together. "Things will bounce back."

"There are ups and downs, and then, there are downs and more downs," he drawls.

Anger thuds at my temples. *I will not lose my temper. I will not.*

He slides his hand into his pocket. "Not that I don't understand your reluctance to sell out."

"You do?"

"Of course. You've invested your sweat and blood, and likely, your entire savings into the venture. Too bad you didn't have a financial person advising you."

Of course, he'd say that. Nate's always been a numbers whiz. I heard that from Ben. It's why, even when they were in the

Marines together, Nate oversaw strategy. He was the person coming up with the game plan for their team. It was Nate's sharp brain which helped them both stay ahead of the enemy; or so my brother informed me over the years. Too bad his best friend's temperament leaves much to be desired.

"I would be willing to consider a merger instead of an acquisition of your little business." His gaze flicks about the place and back at me.

"*Little* business?" I curl my fingers into fists. *Breathe, count back from ten. Do not give into the impulsive need to throw a pie in his face.*

He wipes his thumb under his lip, a considering look in his eyes. "Of course, I don't have to do anything. But given you're Ben's little sister, and he wouldn't want me to leave you in the lurch, I might have a proposition that could help both of us."

"Of course you do."

My sarcasm is lost on him, for he looks me up and down. "Marry me."

To find out what happens next read Skylar & Nathan's story in The Unwanted Wife BY L. STEELE

Or download using this QR code

How to get your physical copy in 60 seconds:

1 **Open your camera:** Point your phone's camera at the QR code as if you're taking a photo.

2 **Tap the link:** A link will pop up on your screen. Tap it to land directly on the book's Amazon page.

3 **Select "Paperback":** Before you hit buy, make sure the **Paperback** format is selected (it's the one that feels best in your hands).

4 **One-Click Buy:** Tap "**Buy now**" to send a fresh copy to your doorstep.

5 **Check your mail:** Keep an eye on your porch! Your new escape is officially en route and will be waiting for you in just a few days.

6 **Happy reading:** Get cozy, crack the spine, and enjoy that "new book" smell. (And maybe set an alarm, because "just one more chapter" is a dangerous game). 📖

READING ORDER

Here's your exclusive L. Steele reading order bingo card

Did you know all the characters you read about have their own book? Cross off their stories as you read and share your bingo card in L. Steele's reader group here

MARRIAGE OF CONVENIENCE BILLIONAIRE ROMANCE FROM L. STEELE

The Billionaire's Fake Wife - Sinclair and Summer's story that started this universe... with a plot twist you won't see coming!

The Billionaire's Secret - Victoria and Saint's story. Saint is maybe the most alphahole of them all!

Marrying the Billionaire Single Dad - Damian and Julia's story, watch out for the plot twist!

The Proposal - Liam and Isla's story. What's a wedding planner to do when you tell the bride not to go through with the wedding and the groom demands you take her place and give him a heir? And yes plot twist!

CHRISTMAS ROMANCE BOOKS BY L. STEELE FOR YOU

Want to find out how Dr. Weston Kincaid and Amelie met? Read The Billionaire's Christmas Bride HERE

Want even more Christmas Romance books? *Read A very Mafia Christmas, Christian and Aurora's story HERE*

Read a marriage of convenience billionaire Christmas romance, Hunter and Zara's story - *The Christmas One Night Stand HERE*

FORBIDDEN BILLIONAIRE ROMANCE BY L. STEELE FOR YOU

Read Daddy JJ's, age-gap romance in Mafia Lust HERE

Read Edward, Baron and Ava's story starting with Billionaire's Sins HERE

ABOUT THE AUTHOR

Hello, I'm L. Steele.

I write romance stories with strong powerful men who meet their match in sassy, curvy, spitfire women.

I love to push myself with each book on both the spice and the angst so I can deliver well rounded, multidimensional characters.

I enjoy trading trivia with my husband, watching lots and lots of movies, and walking nature trails.